WHY THIS IS AN EASY READER

- This story has been carefully written to keep the young reader's interest high.

- It is told in a simple, open style, with a strong rhythm that adds enjoyment both to reading aloud and silent reading.

- There is a very high percentage of words repeated. It is this skillful repetition which helps the child to read independently. Seeing words again and again, he "practices" the vocabulary he knows, and learns with ease the words that are new.

- Only 162 different words have been used, with plurals and root words counted once.

  More than one-half of the words in this story have been used at least three times.

  Over one-fourth of the words in this story have been used at least six times.

  Some words have been used 20, 27 and 56 times.

ABOUT THIS STORY

- There is an important combination here of the familiar and the unfamiliar. The young reader isn't likely to see a baby kangaroo in his world, but he can understand and sympathize with Joey's emotions—and enjoy the satisfying conclusion. This story can be a good "hopping-off" point for the study of less familiar animals. Youngsters will enjoy learning, incidentally, that a baby kangaroo is called a joey.

Too Many Pockets

Story *by* DOROTHY LEVENSON

Pictures *by* RUTH WOOD

Editorial Consultant: LILIAN MOORE

WONDER BOOKS

1107 Broadway, New York 10, N. Y.

Introduction

These books are meant to help the young reader discover what a delightful experience reading can be. The stories are such fun that they urge the child to try his new reading skills. They are so easy to read that they will encourage and strengthen him as a reader.

The adult will notice that the sentences aren't too long, the words aren't too hard, and the skillful repetition is like a helping hand. What the child will feel is: "This is a good story—and I can read it myself!"

For some children, the best way to meet these stories may be to hear them read aloud at first. Others, who are better prepared to read on their own, may need a little help in the beginning—help that is best given freely. Youngsters who have more experience in reading alone—whether in first or second or third grade—will have the immediate joy of reading "all by myself."

These books have been planned to help all young readers grow—in their pleasure in books and in their power to read them.

Lilian Moore
Specialist in Reading
Formerly of Division of Instructional Research,
New York City Board of Education

Joey was a baby kangaroo.

He lived in his mother's pocket.

The pocket was warm and soft—
just right for sleeping and growing.

That's what Joey did
most of the time—sleep and grow.
But sometimes he liked to stand
up in the pocket and look out.

One day Joey was standing up and
looking around.

"What's that out there?" he asked.

"That," said his mother,

"is the world."

Joey looked out at the world.

He saw grass
and trees
and kangaroos.
He saw the kangaroos go
hop

hop

hop

over the grass and under the trees.

"I want to see the world,"

said Joey.

"There it is," said his mother.
"Look around."

"Oh, no," said Joey.
"I want to get out
of this old pocket.
I want to get out
and see the world."

"No, Joey," said his mother.
"Get back into my pocket.
You must be bigger
before you get out."

"Bigger! Bigger! That's all
you tell me," said Joey.
"I am bigger. See! There is
no more room in this pocket."

14

"Joey," said his mother,
"stop jumping around like that!
There is room if you sit still."

"Sit still! Sit still!" said Joey.
"That's all you tell me.
Do I have to sit still in this
pocket all my life?"

15

"Soon you will be bigger,"
said his mother.
"Then you can get out."

"Bigger! Bigger!" said Joey.

"But I want to see the world NOW."

"Joey," said his mother,

"sit still. Go to sleep."

"Go to sleep! That's all

you tell me," said Joey.

"I am NOT sleepy."

One day Joey was looking out

of the pocket.

He looked around.

His mother was eating grass.

18

"I am going to get out
of this old pocket,"
Joey said to himself.
"I am going to get out
right NOW!"

Out came Joey's feet.

Out came his tail.

Out came Joey—

out on the grass.

"Ouch!" said Joey.

The grass was not soft.

But Joey was happy.

"Now I will hop," he said.

Hop.

Hop.

Down went Joey.

He hopped again.

Down he went again.

"Ouch!" said Joey.

The grass was NOT soft.

Joey hopped again.

Down he went again.

Hop. Hop.

This time he did not fall!

This time he went

hop

hop

hop

over the grass and under the trees.

His mother did not see him
hop away.
She was still eating grass.

Joey had fun.

He went hopping all around—

here and there.

It was fun to see the world.

Then Joey sat down.

He looked around for his mother.

But he did not see her.

"I need a pocket," said Joey.

Joey hopped on, looking for
a pocket.

He went

hop

hop

hop

over the grass and under the trees.

He hopped all the way to the farm.

There was the farmer's wife.

"Oh, good!" said Joey.

"I see a pocket."

The farmer's wife had a big pocket.

It looked warm and soft.

So Joey went

hop

hop

into the pocket.

Joey did not know there was

something in the pocket.

Crack! Crack!

Squash! Squash!

Squish! Squish!

"Eeeeeeek!" said the farmer's wife.

Hop! Hop!

Joey was out of that pocket.

Hop! Hop!

Away he went.

"That was not a good pocket!"
said Joey.

Then Joey looked around.

He saw a boy and a girl.

The boy had a big school bag.

"Oh, good!" said Joey.

"I see a pocket."

Joey went

hop

hop

into the bag.

"What's this?" said Joey.

"I don't need this."

"What's this?" said Joey.
"I don't need this
or this."

"What's this?" said Joey.

"I do like this
and this
and this."

The boy got on the bus.

So did Joey!

Bump, bump, bump

went the school bus.

It was a good ride.

It was like a ride

in his mother's pocket.

So Joey went to sleep.

Joey woke up.

He looked around.

Boys and girls.

Girls and boys.

Then someone said,
"Sit still. Sit still,
boys and girls."

"Sit still?" said Joey. "Oh, no!
I have to get out of here."

He hopped out of the bag.

"Oh, look!" said a boy.

"A kangaroo! A baby kangaroo!"

Joey hopped out the door.

"Come back!" the boys

and girls said.

"Come back, kangaroo!"

But away went Joey.

He did not want to sit still.

Hop.

Hop.

Hop went Joey

under some big trees.

Then he saw a truck.

It was standing by a tree.

"Oh, good!" said Joey.

"I see a pocket!"

Hop.

Hop.

Into the pocket went Joey.

Then the truck began to go.

Bump, bump, bump.

It was a good ride.

But the pocket was not soft.

"What's this?" said Joey.

"I don't need this."

"What's this?" said Joey.

"I don't need this

or this

or this!"

The truck went on its way.

The mailman did not see what Joey

was doing.

But the farmer did.

So did the farmer's wife.

The farmer ran after the truck.

The farmer's wife ran after

the farmer.

"Look! Look!" they called

to the mailman.

Joey saw the farmer's wife.

He did not want to get into her

pocket again.

Hop!

Away went Joey under the trees
and over the grass.

"I need a pocket," said Joey.
"I need a warm soft pocket
with nothing in it but me."
Joey saw some kangaroos
in the grass.

Then he saw his mother.

"Joey, Joey!" said his mother.
"Where did you go?"

"I went out to see the world,"
said Joey.

"Oh," said his mother.
"And what is the world like?"

"Well," said Joey, "the world
is full of pockets. But the pockets
are full of things. I did not see
one pocket in the world
with room for just ME!"

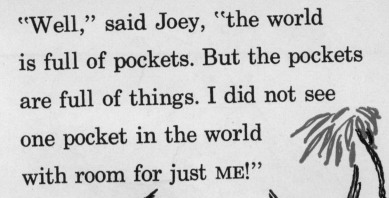

"The best pocket in the world
is right here," Joey said.
"Then jump in," said his mother.
And that's just what Joey did.

CHOOSE FROM THESE EASY READERS

5901 Will You Come to My Party?
5902 Hurry Up, Slowpoke
5903 Mr. Pine's Mixed-up Signs
5904 The Adventures of Silly Billy
5905 The Secret Cat
5906 Billy Brown Makes Something Grand
5907 Miss Polly's Animal School
5908 The Duck on the Truck
5909 A Train for Tommy
5910 Surprise in the Tree
5911 The Monkey in the Rocket
5912 Billy Brown: The Baby Sitter
5913 Fly-Away at the Air Show
5914 Arty the Smarty
5915 The Surprising Pets of Billy Brown
5916 Barney Beagle
5917 I Made a Line
5918 Laurie and the Yellow Curtains
5919 Grandpa's Wonderful Glass
5920 Benjamin in the Woods
5921 Barney Beagle Plays Baseball
5922 The Day Joe Went to the Supermarket
5923 Question and Answer Book
5924 Jokes and Riddles
5925 Let Papa Sleep!
5926 The Surprise in the Story Book
5927 The Big Green Thing
5928 The Boy Who Fooled the Giant
5929 More Jokes and Riddles
5930 Too Many Pockets
5931 The Clumsy Cowboy
5932 Cat in the Box